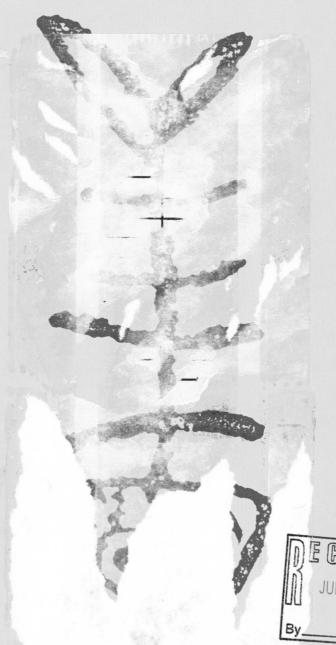

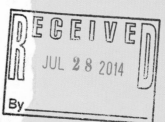

Dog
and
Cat

Ricardo **Alcantara**   Illustrated by **Gusti**

Dog
and
Cat

M
A MILLBROOK PRESS
LIBRARY EDITION

Charles
and Charlotte
were twins.
On their ninth
birthday, their
parents decided
to give them a
special gift.
For Charlotte—
a dog.
For Charles—
a cat.

When they saw the dog and cat, Charles and Charlotte

exclaimed excitedly, "Oh, how cute they are!"

When the cat and dog were face-to-face,
they gave each other a nasty look.

Oh, no! It's a dog, thought the cat.
Oh, no! It's a cat, thought the dog.

And each one said to itself, "Never,

but *never,* will I be friends with that little beast."

They could have ignored each other.
But *no*, they didn't *want* to do that.

The cat tried to frighten the dog by
showing its claws. The dog answered
by growling and baring its teeth.

While the children were busy playing, the cat

swatted the dog's tail with its claws.

Patiently, the dog waited for the right
moment to strike back.

A pan of water was on the floor. *Plop!* The dog jumped in and then shook the water off—all over the cat.

To get even, the cat hid the dog's food.
Then the dog got revenge by drinking the cat's milk.

All day long they took turns
being mean to each other.

Then, little by little, night fell.

Before going to bed, Charles, Charlotte,
and their parents turned out the lights.

The dog and the cat were in the dark.

It was their first night away from their
mothers and they felt very, very scared.

They were both so scared that they trembled from the tips of their ears to the ends of their tails. They didn't dare move as they looked, with big, frightened eyes, at the great black night all around them.

In the darkness each one

saw the glowing eyes of an enemy.

That did it!
Without even thinking about it,
they ran toward one another.
They snuggled up very close to each
other—and, somehow, after a while,
they drifted off to sleep, not so afraid of
the night anymore.

ABOUT THE AUTHOR AND ILLUSTRATOR

Ricardo Alcantara has dedicated his life to the work he loves most: making up stories. He has been writing for children for more than twenty years and has published more than a hundred books, many of which have won awards. He lives in Barcelona, Spain.

Gusti has worked as an animator for movies and cartoons, but now specializes in illustrating posters and award-winning books for children. When he is not drawing, Gusti likes playing music and training birds of prey. He lives in Barcelona, Spain.

Library of Congress Cataloging-in-Publication Data
Alcantara, Ricardo.
(Chien et chat. English)
Dog and cat / Ricardo Alcantara ; illustrated by Gusti ;
(translation by Elizabeth Uhlig).
p. cm.
Summary: A dog and a cat living in the same household
attempt to make each other's life miserable but only until
night comes, the family goes to bed, and fear sets in.
ISBN 0-7613-1420-2 (lib. ed.)
(l. Cats—Fiction. 2. Dogs—Fiction.) I. Rosemffet, Gustavo,
ill. II. Uhlig, Elizabeth. III. Title.
PZ7.A326Do 1999 (E)—dc21 98-29896 CIP AC

First published in the United States
by The Millbrook Press, Inc.
2 Old New Milford Road
Brookfield, Connecticut 06804

First published in France by
Hachette Jeunesse under the title
CHIEN ET CHAT

Translation by Elizabeth Uhlig

Copyright © 1998 Hachette Livres
English translation © 1999 The Millbrook Press

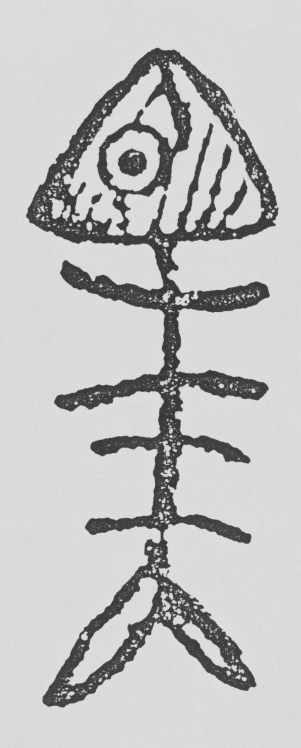